THE
MASTER'S
BRICK

MELISA BASS O'CONNOR
Illustrated by Marcia O'Connor

ISBN: 978-1-4497-5645-1

WestBow Press books may be ordered through booksellers or by contacting:

WestBow Press
A Division of Thomas Nelson
1663 Liberty Drive
Bloomington, IN 47403
www.westbowpress.com
1-(866) 928-1240

Printed in the United States of America

Library of Congress Control Number: 2012910891

WestBow Press rev. date: 10/22/2012

WESTBOW
PRESS
A DIVISION OF THOMAS NELSON

Acknowledgements

There are some wonderful people who were very instrumental in the production of this book.

Craig Richards, thank you for allowing me to run with your idea!

Myrtle Bass Bradley, you have always enjoyed and encouraged my writings. Thank you, Momma!

And last, but certainly not least, Benjamin O'Connor and Marcia O'Connor, I love the way the two of you collaborated to come up with such beautiful illustrations. We make a great team. I look forward to working with you again in the near future!

Book Dedication

The unconditional love, support, and encouragement I receive from my husband is priceless. Benjamin, it is a blessing to be your wife and best friend. Thank you for dreaming with me.

Long ago, there lived a kind brick maker. He made the most wonderful bricks. They were strong bricks, made with the purist red clay. Every brick was perfect in its own way, because the brick maker lovingly shaped and molded each one to be so. He spoke to the clay as he worked it with his hands. "What wonderful clay you are," he would say. As he fired the clay he would say, "Oh look at you! What a strong brick you are becoming." And then, when the brick was finally complete, he would say, "Oh, you beautiful brick! What a splendid purpose you were created for!" The brick maker loved each of his creations, and in return, they loved their master.

One day, the master made an especially fine brick. "I am very pleased with you," he said. "You are very important and have been created for a most wonderful purpose! There is a shepherd who is building a warm stable in which to keep his lambs. Tomorrow we shall travel along with your brothers to your destiny!"

Well, the brick was very excited that the Master was so pleased with him. When the Master placed him with the others, he began to boast about how special he was.

"I am the most perfect brick the Master has ever created," he said.

"Oh yes," replied one of the other bricks. "We can see that you are very fine indeed. You must have been created for the King's new palace gate."

This made the little brick think. Surely the Master would offer such a beautiful brick as he to the king! There must have been a mistake! After all, he was the most perfect brick ever and it would be a waste to use such a wonderful work in a simple stable.

Early the next morning, the Master carefully loaded the bricks onto a cart. After making sure that each one was safely in place he said, "Today, my sons, we go forth to your destiny!" Then the Master and his bricks set off down the road.

"I wonder which part of the stable I will be used in?" said one of the brothers.

"Oh, we are not going to be in a stable," said the perfect brick. "We are on our way to the king's palace."

"Oh no, replied the brother. "The Master said we were specifically made for that wonderful new stable! Isn't it exciting?"

"Maybe for you," replied the perfect brick. "However, I was made for a more important purpose. A stable would not do for a brick such as me! I am far too fine for such a humble building. Oh, how splendid the king's palace gate will look once I am in place!"

The perfect brick got so lost in his thinking, that he almost didn't notice the grand structure they were passing. "Wait!" cried the brick. "This is my stop! This is the king's palace! This is my destiny!" The Master, however, just kept on riding. "He is going to pass right by my destiny because he can't hear me!" thought the perfect brick. "Maybe if I move, I can get his attention!"

And so, the perfect brick tried to move. He tried and tried, but his sides were so perfectly square that he just could not move. "Help me!" he cried to his brothers. "If you don't help me, I will miss my destiny!"

So, the other bricks all worked together to help the perfect brick. They squeezed and wiggled until the perfect brick was finally pushed to the very edge of the cart.

"More, more!" cried the perfect brick!

"That is all we can do, brother!" replied the other bricks. "If we get closer, we will fall with you to your destiny and miss our own!"

"But don't you see?" said the perfect brick. "My destiny is more important than yours! You must help me!"

But the brothers did nothing else to help. And, just as the perfect brick thought all was lost, the cart's wheel hit a rut in the road, which sent him flying from the cart.

"Goodbye brother," called the other bricks. "We wish you well!"

"Well, indeed!" thought the perfect brick as he hit the ground.

"They will see how important I am!" he thought as he tumbled to a stop right by the side of the gate, where he waited to be placed into his destiny.

He waited and he waited. And, then when he thought he could wait no more, a builder picked him up.

 "What about this brick?" the builder asked.

"That's a nice brick," said another builder, "but see that tiny crack? You will have to cover it with mortar."

The brick was shocked! A crack? It must have happened when he hit the ground. But, the man said it was tiny and could be covered. He could still be used in the gate, for sure.

Covering the brick with thick, wet mortar, the man said, "I'll put this one down here, where it won't be as noticeable." And then, he pushed the brick into a very tight spot just above the ground.

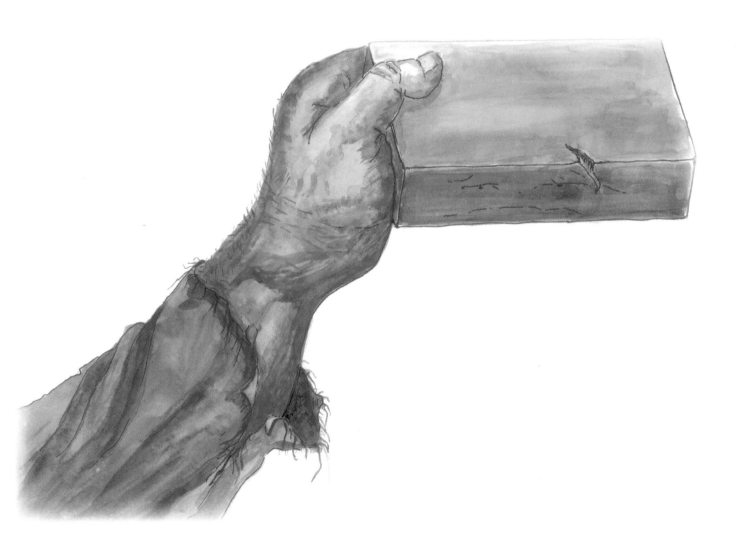

"What!" said the brick? "Not as noticeable? Can't he see my fine quality? Why, I am perfect!"

"Yes," said another brick in the gate. "Perfectly big, if you ask me."

"A little too big," said another. "You look nothing like the rest of us. You are in the wrong place."

"Yes, yes!" said the perfect brick. "Finally, someone understands me! I am too fine to be way down here! I need to be higher, where the king can see me!

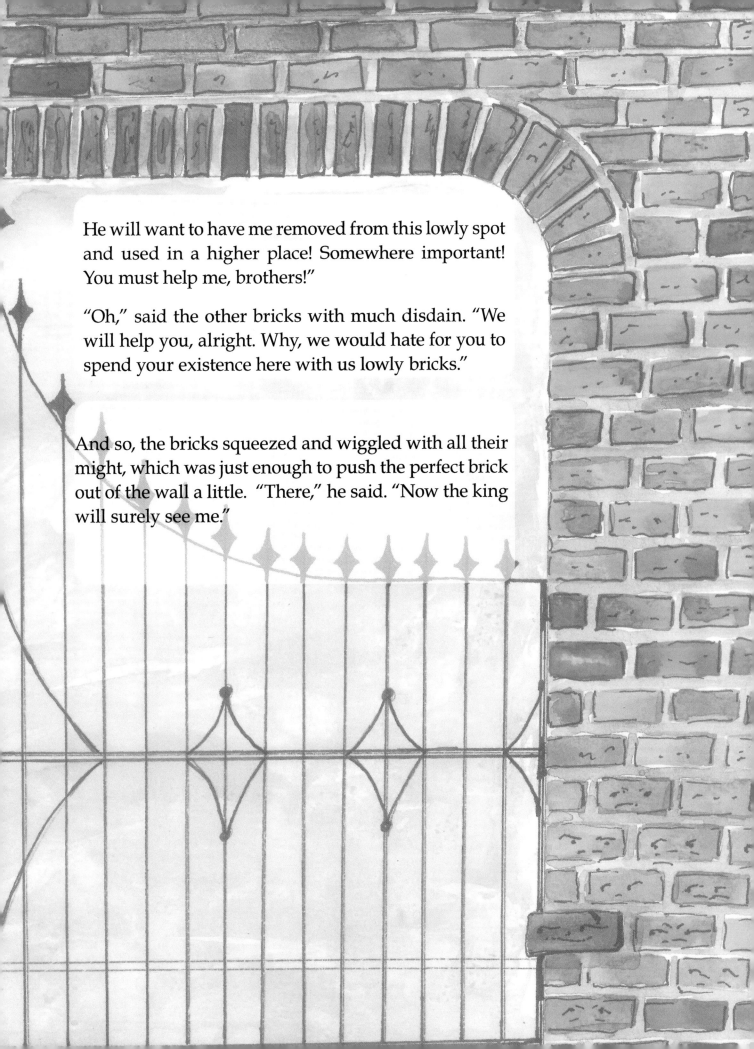

He will want to have me removed from this lowly spot and used in a higher place! Somewhere important! You must help me, brothers!"

"Oh," said the other bricks with much disdain. "We will help you, alright. Why, we would hate for you to spend your existence here with us lowly bricks."

And so, the bricks squeezed and wiggled with all their might, which was just enough to push the perfect brick out of the wall a little. "There," he said. "Now the king will surely see me."

So, there he waited for the king to see him. He waited and he waited. And then, when he thought he could wait no more, the king arrived. As he passed by, he stopped to have a look at his new gate. Something did not seem right. His gaze fell on a brick at the bottom of the gate. "See that brick," he said to one of the builders. "That brick is not right for that spot. It needs to be removed."

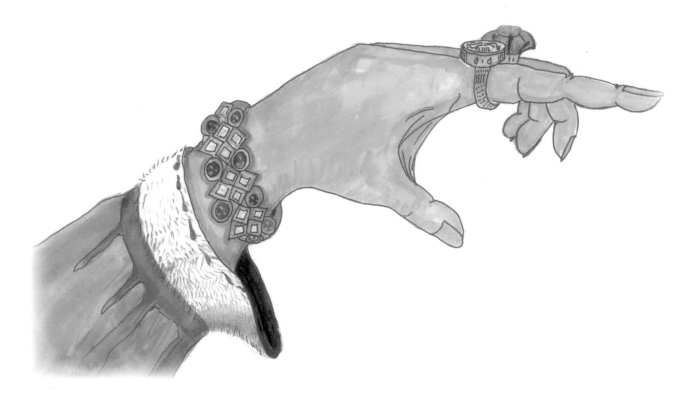

"Where should I put it, Your Highness?" asked the builder.
"Finally!" thought the brick! Now is my time to shine! Yes, tell him, Your Highness! Tell him where I belong!

After some thought the king finally said, "I do not think this brick belongs at all. It is too big…bigger than the other bricks. And see here? Is that a tiny crack? No, no, no! It will not do! I will not, cannot have a cracked brick anywhere in my palace gate! Remove it at once!"

"No," gasped the brick! "I am perfect, I am perfect! The king is surely mistaken!"

"No," said the other bricks. "The king has made no mistake. You even said yourself that you did not belong in such a lowly place."

As the builder began to chip and dig at the dry, hard mortar, the brick cried out. "Help me brothers! Hold on to me! Do not let go of me!"

"We cannot," said the other bricks. "If we hold on to you, we may be pulled away with you, away from our destiny. We are sorry, but we wish you well, brother."

"Well, indeed" said the brick, as he felt his once perfect sides being chipped and cracked by the builder. "What is to become of me? Of what importance am I now?" asked the brick, as the builder tossed him to the rubbish heap. "Well, indeed."

Seasons came and went, and all the while the once perfect brick laid there in the grass by the rubbish heap.

Lonely, he thought of his brothers. They must be happy together, fulfilling their purpose.

Crushed, he thought of the king, who must be happy with his new palace gate.

Broken, he thought of the Master.

"Master!" cried the brick. "How disappointed you would be if you could see me now! How could I have had such little faith in you? Oh Master, you knew me and loved me. Please come for me! Please save me!"

There the brick waited, and waited and waited.

He waited in the day. He waited in the night.

He waited in his sorrow. He waited in his pain.

And finally, when he thought he could wait no more, he continued to wait.

Suddenly, just as the brick thought he was lost forever, he felt lightness. It was as if…as if he was…

Yes! It was! He was being picked up. These hands, he knew these hands. So hard, so calloused….so loving.

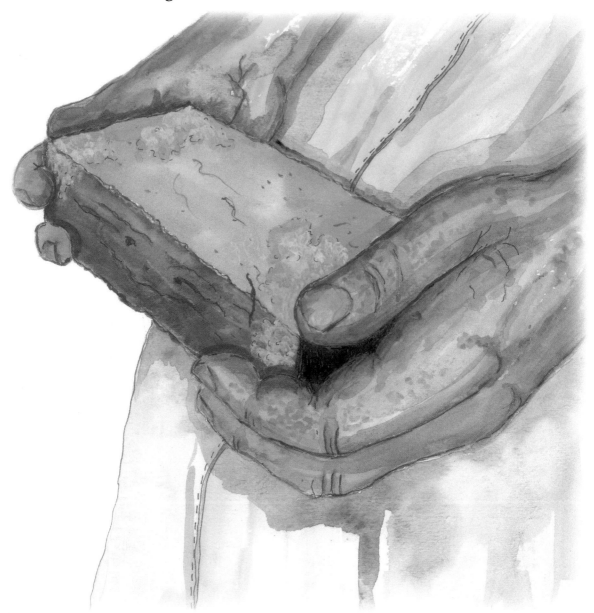

"Oh, Master! You came! Please, do not see what I have become," the brick cried with shame. Yet, the Master held his brick. It was scratched, and cracked. It was dirty and covered with hard mortar.

The master cradled his creation. And, in his most loving voice, he said, "There you are. I have been looking for you. I have missed you. Your brothers have missed you. You have a purpose to fulfill. Let us go home and make you ready."

So, the Master carried his brick home. As he washed the brick he said to it, "Oh, what a wonderful brick you are." As he sanded the brick he said, "Oh, what a strong brick you are." And as he polished the brick he said, "What a wonderful purpose you were created for, Beloved. Tomorrow, we shall travel to your destiny."

Early the next morning, the Master tucked his beloved brick into a safe place on the cart. "Today is a wonderful day for purpose," he said. And taking up the reins, they set off down the road.

As they passed the King's palace gate, the brick looked at the small bricks in the wall. How beautiful they were! Why, each one fit perfectly into its own space, as if it were created just for that spot! He called out them, "I wish you well, my brothers! How splendid you look in your destiny!"

Together, the brick and his Master rode on until they reached a small bend in the road. "We are almost there, beloved," said the Master. "Your brothers have been eagerly awaiting your arrival. The winds will soon turn cold and there is a newborn lamb in the stable. You were made for such a time as this."

The brick could see the little building now. It was not as grand as the palace gate, but it was every bit as lovely! As they drew closer, the brick looked at the other bricks in the stable. How beautiful they were! Why, each one fit perfectly into its own space, as if it were created just for that spot! He called out to them, "Hello brothers!"

"Hello, indeed!" they replied! "Welcome home, brother!"

The master took his brick from the cart. With great care, he slid the brick into an open spot in the wall. It was a perfect fit! It was the spot he was created for "Serve your purpose well, my beloved." said the brick master. "I will see you again, soon."

How wonderful the brick felt to be amongst his brothers again. How splendid it was to fulfill his purpose. And as he watched his master kneeling inside the simple stable to admire the newborn lamb, he knew that he would indeed serve his purpose well. Well indeed!